JASON STRANGE

Zombie Winter

Cover Illustration by Serg Soleiman

Interior Illustration by Phil Parks

STONE ARCH BOOKS
a capstone imprint

Jason Strange is published by Stone Arch Books
A Capstone Imprint
151 Good Counsel Drive, P.O. Box 669
Mankato, Minnesota 56002
www.capstonepub.com

Copyright © 2011 by Stone Arch Books

Library of Congress Cataloging-in-Publication Data is available on the Library of Congress website.

Library Binding: 978-1-4342-2964-9
Paperback: 978-1-4342-3095-9
Paperback: 978-1-4342-3999-0

Summary: Which is worse—a long, cold winter, or a town of zombies?

Art Director/Graphic Designer: Kay Fraser
Production Specialist: Michelle Biedscheid

Photo credits:
Shutterstock: Nikita Rogul (handcuffs, p. 2); Stephen Mulcahey (police badge, p. 2); B&T Media Group (blank badge, p. 2); Picsfive (coffee stain, pp. 2, 5, 12, 17, 24, 30, 42, 48, 57); Andy Dean Photography (paper, pen, coffee, pp. 2, 66); osov (blank notes, p. 1); Thomas M Perkins (folder with blank paper, pp. 66, 67); M.E. Mulder (black electrical tape, pp. 69, 70, 71)

Printed in China.
052011   005193

TABLE OF CONTENTS

- Chapter 1: **The Long Winter** -

By the beginning of February, Kane Tuttle was sick of winter. He was sick of walking to school before the sun was up, and he was sick of gray skies all day. He was sick of having to walk through six new inches of snow a few times every week.

Kane kept his hood on and his head down. He kept his hands shoved into the pockets of his heavy winter coat. His feet crunched along the snowy path toward Ravens Pass Middle School.

Kane stopped at the corner of Forest Road. From down the street, a lone figure was walking toward him. It moved slowly, like Kane had been. Then it raised a hand. Kane waved back. It was his friend Nick Ellis. Kane and Nick always walked to school together from that corner. Kane didn't mind waiting, even though it was cold. After all, it was always cold.

If you walked a few blocks down Forest the other way from Nick's house, you came to the old Ravenswood forest. Those were the woods the town was named after. Everyone said Ravens Pass was built as a safe way to get past the Ravenswood forest.

Some of the kids at school said a hermit lived in those woods. They said he'd been living there since before the town was even built.

Kane didn't know if that was true, but he did know that Ravens Pass was more than three hundred years old. No one could live that long, even alone in the woods.

"Hey," Nick said when he reached Kane.

"Hey," Kane mumbled back. He pulled his wool hat further down over his ears. Together, the two boys plodded on toward the school. By the time they reached the old brick building, they were dragging their feet, and their heads hung low.

– Chapter 2: **Cure for Grumps** –

Kane and Nick moved slowly through the halls. Kane didn't even pull his hood off until he got to his locker.

All of the other students at Ravens Pass Middle School also had their hoods on. They walked through the halls to their lockers with their heads down.

"Boy, everyone sure is grumpy today," a man's voice said loudly. It was Mr. Theodore, the librarian.

Kane nodded. Then he put his hat, coat, and gloves into his locker and found his math book. He grabbed it and shut the locker.

"I guess you're grumpy, too," Mr. Theodore said. "These winters sure are tough, huh? Long and cold."

"I guess," Kane said. Then he walked off toward homeroom. He met up with Nick. Among the crowd of slow-moving students, the two boys dragged themselves through the halls.

Kane knew Mr. Theodore wasn't trying to be a jerk. He wasn't a bad guy; he just wasn't from Ravens Pass. He was from someplace down south where they hardly had winter at all. To him, a long snowy Ravens Pass winter was still kind of fun, like it had been for Kane when he was a little boy.

Back then, he and Nick would have gone sledding, built forts and snowmen, had huge snowball fights. But not now. Now the winter drained every ounce of energy from him. He just felt dead tired most of the time.

As the students in Kane's homeroom slid into their seats, Principal Drone's voice rang out on the loudspeaker. "Good morning, students," he said slowly. He sounded as tired as Kane felt. "Just a few announcements this morning."

The principal announced the normal stuff. Math club meetings, a library book sale, and a track meet canceled due to snow.

Kane stared at the homeroom teacher, Mr. Hackenbush. He was sitting at the desk in front of class, one hand on a mug of something with lots of foam on top — some kind of fancy coffee drink.

But his head was down on the desk. If his back hadn't been moving up and down to show he was breathing, Kane would have thought Mr. Hackenbush was dead.

"And one more announcement," the principal said. "Our new lunch lady, Ms. Garrity, has come up with a great idea to lift all our spirits. Today at lunch, free hot cocoa for everyone!"

Mr. Hackenbush lifted his head an inch before dropping it back on his desk.

"Huh," Kane said. Nick nodded.

A couple of other kids said, "Hm," and "Ah."

It was the most excitement Kane had seen at school for months.

Kane wasn't excited, though. He was allergic to chocolate.

~ Chapter 3: **Three Late Students** ~

It was a long morning. Kane spent most of math class staring out the window at the gray and white sky and the snow-covered fields.

After a while, his eyes felt numb. He could hardly hear the teacher as he rambled slowly on about algebra. Instead, Kane only heard the humming and rattling of the heaters under the metal grates near the back of the room.

When three people appeared, lumbering toward the school from across the athletic field, Kane didn't notice at first. But after a minute, he thought, *Who are those guys? They're walking so slow.*

As they got closer, Kane squinted across the field of white snow. The figures were wearing hoods, like everyone else in Ravens Pass in February. But they moved so oddly. Their heads were down — that wasn't weird. But these guys' heads seemed even lower than most people in Ravens Pass.

And their feet. They were sort of dragging their feet instead of walking.

"Huh," Kane said. He was so tired, he accidentally said it out loud.

"Is something outside interesting, Kane?" the teacher asked in a worn-out voice.

Kane looked toward the front of the room. "Not really, Mr. Green," he said. "Just these three guys. I think they're in eighth grade. They must be late for school, but they aren't hurrying."

The rest of the class and Mr. Green glanced out the window for a moment. "They look like they're half dead," the teacher said in his low voice. Then he closed the blinds.

"There," he said. "Now you won't be distracted by the excitement."

Kane put his head down and listened to the clock. It ticked slowly toward lunchtime.

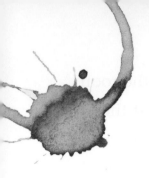

– Chapter 4: **Too Crowded** –

Kane walked slowly to the cafeteria when lunch finally rolled around. Nick met him just outside the cafeteria, along with their other good friend, Hank.

"Free hot chocolate today," Hank said. Nick and Kane nodded. "I hope it's good," Hank added. "A good cup of hot chocolate would be great right about now."

Kane shrugged. "I don't care if it's good," he said. "I can't have any anyway."

"Okay, Mr. Allergic to Everything," Nick joked. The three boys pushed through the big double doors into the cafeteria.

Then they stopped in their tracks.

The cafeteria was a madhouse. Students were pushing toward the food line, moaning and shrieking, reaching out their arms.

"What's going on here?" Kane said, his face wrinkled with confusion.

Nick shook his head. "I guess the hot cocoa must be good," he said.

He found a sixth grader near the back of the group and grabbed his shirt, pulling him around to face him.

"What's all the chaos about?" Nick asked.

The sixth grader looked at him with empty, wide eyes.

His mouth hung open, and from it dripped dark brown liquid. It oozed over his lip and down his chin. He didn't say anything. Nick took a step back.

"Wow," Kane said. "I guess he really likes the cocoa."

Hank nodded. "Looks like everyone does," he said. Then he looked at Nick and smiled. "I gotta get me some of that!"

Nick smiled, and he and Hank high-fived. Kane just laughed. "Enjoy," he said. "I'm taking my lunch to the library to eat in peace. This place is nuts."

Kane turned around. He pulled open the double doors and entered the eerie quiet of the hallway. As he headed toward the library, he passed the back way into the cafeteria — the door that teachers used.

He peeked through the door's window and saw Ms. Garrity, the new lunch lady. She was standing over a huge pot of bubbling brown liquid, stirring it slowly, and smiling.

– Chapter 5: **Too Quiet** –

The library was silent when Kane walked in. "Mr. Theodore?" Kane said. He walked up to the counter near the front of the library.

But there was no one there. The library was completely quiet.

"Mr. Theodore is probably in the cafeteria, too," Kane muttered to himself. He headed to the comics section. A new issue of *Undeath* was out, and Kane was dying to read it.

When Kane reached the comics shelves, he saw three eighth graders gathered close together in front of the racks. Their backs were to him, but they seemed to be looking at something together. From their dark hoodies, he could tell they were the same three guys he'd seen from the window of his math class.

"Hey, is that the new issue of *Undeath*?" Kane said, stepping up to them. "I can't wait to read it. I was hoping to look at it while I ate my lunch."

None of the three boys turned around. They didn't even move.

"Um, hello?" Kane said. He moved a little closer and put a hand on one of their shoulders.

Swish!

All three turned at once and stared at him. Kane jumped back. Their eyes were deep and dark. Their faces were pale and gaunt, except right under their chins. There, a dark brown stain dripped from their mouths and chins.

"Unnnhhh," they said together. They moved toward him.

Kane took a quick step back. "Um, are you guys okay?" he said. "What are you —"

Then he saw. The three eighth graders hadn't been looking at any comics. They'd been standing over a person.

"Mr. Theodore!" Kane shouted. The librarian lay in a crumpled heap, barely moving.

"Kane . . . ," the librarian said. He strained to lift his head.

Mr. Theodore's clothes and face were stained with the brown liquid, too, but there wasn't any near his mouth. "Run!" Mr. Theodore said. Then he dropped to the floor.

Kane stared for a minute at the fallen librarian, then at the three eighth graders. One of them reached for him. Kane leaped back.

"Whoa," he said quietly. Then he turned and ran for the door.

– Chapter 6: **The Mob** –

Just as Kane slammed through the swinging library doors, the bell rang. Lunch was over.

The cafeteria doors opened with a bang. Kane stopped dead. A horde of students and teachers came pouring out of the cafeteria.

There were hundreds of them. In an instant, the hallway was full. When one of them saw Kane, they all stopped and looked at him.

Their faces were all covered in dripping chocolate.

"Unnnnhhhh . . . ," the kid at the front said, pointing at Kane. The rest began to moan and wail, too. They stumbled toward him. Kane turned to run, but the three eighth graders from the library were right behind him.

"Oh no," Kane whispered. He was trapped.

He turned to the big group coming from the cafeteria. They were getting closer.

He put up his hands. "Look, guys," he said. "I don't have any of that hot cocoa. Honest!"

A hand grabbed his shoulder, and Kane spun. It was the new lunch lady. She'd come out of the cafeteria staff entrance.

"Don't worry, sonny," she said. "They don't want cocoa anymore."

"They . . . they don't?" Kane said. He pulled away from her.

She laughed. "Not at all," she said. "Not anymore. Their transformation is complete."

"Transformation?" Kane repeated. He looked around, hoping for any way to escape.

The lunch lady smiled at him, nodding slowly. "The cocoa changed them. Now they are my zombie army," she said. "And now they only eat brains!"

– Chapter 7: **Brains!** –

Kane was surrounded.

An army of student and teacher zombies was coming down on him from one side. Three eighth graders were heading toward him from the library. And the lunch lady — the zombie queen! — was in front of him. He was trapped.

"Give in," the lunch lady said. She held out a steaming cup of cocoa. "Just drink this, and you will live forever in my army."

"No, I can't," Kane said. "I'm allergic to chocolate."

The lunch lady chuckled. "Allergic?" she said through tears of laughter.

Kane squinted at her. "What's so funny?" he asked.

"You're worried about allergies? You should be worrying about your classmates eating your brains!" the lunch lady said, still laughing.

Kane knew he had to do something. He knocked the cup of cocoa from her hand. The hot chocolate spilled all over the school's white tile floor. Then, just as the zombies reached him, he rushed past her through the cafeteria staff door.

Kane ran through the kitchen toward the service line, then to the big double doors.

When he pushed through them into the hall, the mob of zombies was facing the other way. They were looking for him at the staff entrance.

Across the hall was the door to the gym. "Perfect," he said. "No one will be in the gym. I'll escape through there. Then I can get out to the athletic field."

But the gym wasn't empty. At the far end of the basketball court, in front of the hoop, was Nick. He was slowly dribbling a basketball. He looked up at the net like he was getting ready to shoot a free throw.

"Nick!" Kane said, running down the court. "I'm so glad to see you."

Nick stopped dribbling. He picked up the basketball and held it up. But he didn't shoot. He just let the ball fall to the floor.

It bounced across the floor toward the bleachers. The sound echoed through the gym.

"Are you okay?" Kane asked. "You must have left the cafeteria right after I did, huh? Did you see all those crazy people?"

Nick still didn't turn around. He just stood there, staring at the hoop.

"Can you believe what's going on around here?" Kane asked. He jogged over to the basketball and picked it up. "I think I finally lost them. The zombies, I mean. We better call the cops or something, right?"

Nick didn't reply.

"Catch," Kane said. He tossed the ball to his friend.

The ball hit Nick in the shoulder and fell to the floor. Then it rolled against the wall.

Finally Nick turned. He stared through deep, dead eyes. His mouth hung open, and the stain of hot cocoa ran down his chin and the front of his shirt.

"Oh no," Kane said, looking at his friend's face. "You did drink the cocoa, didn't you?"

Nick moaned, "Unnnnhh . . ." Suddenly he lunged at Kane, his hands out in front of him. Nick grabbed for Kane's throat.

"No!" Kane shouted. He shoved Nick to the ground. Then the gym doors flew open.

"There he is!" the lunch lady called to her army. "Don't let him escape!"

Kane didn't wait around to see the army of zombies rush at him. He ran for the doors to the athletic field. He slammed through them into the white, cold outside. The field lay before him, and he ran.

– Chapter 8: **Into the Woods** –

The cold air stung Kane's face and hands. He'd left his coat, hat, and gloves in his locker.

"Too late to worry about that," he said to himself as he ran across the snow-covered field.

The snow was deep enough that running was difficult. With every step his boots got wetter, then his socks, until finally his feet were soaking wet and freezing.

Kane risked a glance over his shoulder. The zombies were in the field, running toward him. He noticed the lunch lady was no longer at the front of the crowd.

"She probably went into town," Kane muttered, "to infect the rest of Ravens Pass."

Looming up in front of Kane was Ravenswood Forest. He had no choice but to go in.

Kane had been inside the forest before, but only a few feet. He'd never gone in far enough to get lost. But now he didn't have a choice.

He could get to Main Street fastest by cutting through the forest. If he could beat the lunch lady to town, he could warn everyone.

As long as he didn't get lost in the forest.

"So," Kane said to himself as he jogged between trees, "Main Street should be on my right. If I just keep in a straight line, I should come out just on the edge of town, at the end of Main Street."

Kane listened to the sound of his feet crunching in the snow as he ran. He did his best to head straight toward Main Street, but the woods were confusing. He had to turn sometimes.

By the time he was a hundred yards into the woods, he was hopelessly lost.

"Great," he said. He stopped to try to get his bearings. "I turned once to go around the creek, and then again at the birch trees. So I should have to go . . ."

Then he heard it.

"Unnnnhhh . . ."

The moaning zombies were still not very close, but they were gaining on him. He picked a direction in the dark forest and ran. Suddenly, he spotted some lights not too far off. "I made it!" he said, running toward the lights. "That must be Main Street."

But it wasn't. After a few steps, Kane realized he was running toward a little shack. A couple of candles burned in the windows.

"It's better than nothing," he told himself. "If I don't hide, the zombies will catch me."

He ran up to the door and knocked. "Is anyone there?" he called out.

There was no answer right away. Kane didn't have time to wait. He pushed the door open and looked around for someplace to hide in the one-room shack.

There was a cellar door in the middle of floor. He pulled it open and hurried down the rickety ladder into a dirt-floor basement.

Kane crouched into the corner and sat, waiting. Before too long, he heard a loud creaking. It sounded like someone had opened the front door. There were heavy steps over his head. Suddenly, a shaft of light came in through the cellar door.

Then a pair of old boots stepped slowly into the cellar.

The Ravenswood hermit.

– Chapter 9: **Mr. Entwhistle** –

"Who's down here?" a voice called out.

Kane held his breath.

"Come out now," the voice said. "Those zombies ran past. You're safe."

Kane stepped out of the darkness.

An old man stood in the middle of the cellar, holding a lit candle. "Don't be afraid," the man said. "My name is Mortimer Entwhistle. I live here."

"Oh," Kane said. "I'm sorry for barging into your house."

The man put his candle down on a table next to a small chair and sat down. "That's okay. I don't blame you," he said.

"You're safe for the moment, like I said," Mortimer went on. "But if zombies want your brains, they'll never give up."

"Never?" Kane repeated, stunned. "So I'm doomed?"

Mortimer took a deep breath and sighed. He leaned forward in his chair. The candle cast long shadows over his face. "Not for sure," he said. "If only we knew who created the zombies."

Kane brightened. "We do!" he said. "The school lunch lady! She's new. Her name is Ms. Garrity."

Mortimer scratched his chin. "Garrity," he said quietly. "Long ago, there was a zombie uprising here in Ravens Pass. Their queen was an old lady who lived deep in these woods," he said. "Deeper even than my shack. Deeper than the bravest travelers dare to go."

The old man stood up and picked up the candle. He walked to the nearest wall and looked at an old photograph. "She was called Bridget O'Garrity."

"Like Ms. Garrity!" Kane said. "Sort of."

"Right," Mortimer said. "But, son, that was back in 1911. A hundred years ago."

Kane squinted at the old man, then at the photo on the wall. It did look like the new lunch lady. "Then it can't be her," he said. "No one can live that long."

Mortimer raised his eyebrow. Then he said, "Here's what you have to do." He returned to his chair and put the candle down again. "To stop the uprising, you must destroy the queen."

"Kill Ms. Garrity?" Kane said.

"Not exactly," Mortimer said. "She can't be killed. She isn't really alive. However, you must destroy her the right way. There's only one way to do it."

"What kind of way?" Kane asked. "Like a wooden stake through the heart? Or a silver bullet?"

"Nothing like that," Mortimer said. "You have to do it the right way, or her army of zombies would turn to dust like that." He snapped his fingers. The pop made Kane jump.

"But we don't want to destroy the zombies," Mortimer said. "We want to save them. And their victims, too. To do that, you must cover the queen with the poison she used to change the zombies."

"The hot cocoa?" Kane said.

Mortimer cocked his head. "Did she use cocoa?" he said. "In 1911 it was gruel. Hardly anyone would eat it. It was a very small uprising."

"Well, this time it's just about every kid at Ravens Pass Middle School," Kane said. "They couldn't get enough of the hot cocoa."

Mortimer nodded. "That settles it," he said. "To save your classmates, you must drown her in the vat of cocoa."

"Okay," Kane said. "Got it. Now I think she's on her way downtown."

Mortimer stood up and walked back to the wall with the photo. "You must warn them. Take my secret tunnel," he said, opening a hidden door.

Kane looked into the tunnel, then at Mortimer. "Really?" he said. "All the way to Main Street?"

Mortimer shrugged. "What?" he said. "Hermits need groceries, too." He handed Kane the candle. "You'll need this," he said. "Now hurry. I fear it might be too late for the town already."

"I'll do my best," Kane said. "Thanks, Mr. Entwhistle."

Kane started down the dark, cold tunnel. He could hardly see, and he had no idea how far he had to go.

– Chapter 10: **Main Street** –

The tunnel was long and hardly tall enough for Kane to walk through without stooping. With every step, he heard the scritching and scratching of mice and rats and who knows what else crawling around him.

Though the candle was big, he could never see more than a few steps in front of him. Several times he walked into the dirt walls of the tunnel when he reached a curve.

After half an hour, Kane reached a complete dead end. He looked around, hoping to find a door like the one Mortimer had opened in the cellar of his shack. Instead, he was surrounded by walls of packed dirt.

Then he noticed the black smoke coming from his giant candle. It was going down, toward the floor.

Kane got down on his knees and felt around until he found a loop of iron. He tugged on it, and a trap door opened. Kane knew he didn't have any other options, so he dropped into the darkness.

The candle fell and went out as he jumped. Then his feet struck something hard, like cement. He banged into something, and there was a crash as dozens of cans fell around him.

Kane fell forward onto a set of steps. He managed to climb them. Then he spotted a sliver of light in front of him. He went toward it. It was a crack of light coming from beneath a swinging door. Kane pushed the door open.

Right away, Kane had to squint and shield his eyes, it was so bright. Once his eyes had adjusted, he realized where he was. He was in the cereal aisle of the supermarket on Main Street. And it was completely empty.

Kane walked quickly through the aisles toward the exit. Even the cash registers were deserted.

The automatic doors slid open, and Kane went out into the street. He had forgotten how cold it was outside. He wished that he had his hat and coat.

"First stop, the bank," Kane said. His mother was a teller there.

The bank was right across Main from the supermarket, so Kane ran across the street.

He burst through the doors of the bank, but it was as empty as the supermarket. "Where is everybody?" he asked the empty room. "There must be thousands of dollars here, and no one's guarding all the money!"

I better go to the police, he thought. He ran up Main Street toward First. But as he rounded the corner he stopped dead.

A huge mob of people was streaming toward him. They were all coming out of the big coffee shop a block away. Every one of them was moaning and limping. Stains of chocolate ran down their faces and shirts. They were zombies. All of them.

– Chapter 11: **Cornered** –

Kane turned to run. *I have to find that lunch lady,* he thought.

But as he sprinted toward school, he came face to face with zombie Nick.

"Unnnnhhhh!" Nick said.

"Nick," Kane said, backing away. "It's me. Your friend!"

Behind Nick, and not very far, were the rest of the middle-school zombies.

Teachers, students, and Principal Drone were walking down Main Street toward the corner of First. Kane was trapped between the two mobs.

If some of them are coming out of the coffee shop, he realized, *then the lunch lady must be in there, making drinks!*

Kane turned and ran toward the mob coming out of the coffee shop. If he hurried, he'd reach the alley that cut from First Street to Second Street before the zombies did.

He ran at top speed toward the zombies. "I'm going to make it," he said to himself as he ran. "So close. . . ."

Then, at the front of the mob of zombies, Kane spotted his mother. She was heading right toward him, but she didn't seem to recognize him.

Her mouth hung open, and she had one arm out in front of him, like she planned to grab him. "Mom! It's me! Kane!" Kane yelled. But she didn't react. "My mom is going to eat my brains," Kane muttered.

He knew what he had to do to save his mom and to save Nick and all his friends from school. He had to stop the lunch lady.

Kane started running again. He reached the alley just in time. He turned sharply to the right just before the zombies could grab him. As the crowd tried to follow him into the alley, they all crumpled together and couldn't get through quickly.

Meanwhile, Kane reached Second Street. He cut left to circle around, back to the coffee shop. A sign on the front of the shop read, "New drinks! Come in for a free sample."

– Chapter 12: **In the Drink** –

Kane barged through the coffee shop doors. A mop was leaning on the wall. He grabbed it, then slid it through the door handles to lock the doors. He knew that at any moment the zombie mobs would both be at the door, trying to finally catch him.

Then he heard a voice. "You!"

Lunchlady Garrity stood behind the counter in the back. She stood over a huge pot of steaming liquid.

"Yup, it's me," Kane said. "Your zombie army still hasn't caught me. I still have my brains."

"Well then," Ms. Garrity said. "I guess you beat me. Would you like a warm drink?"

"Is that your zombie hot cocoa?" Kane said. He moved closer to her, slowly.

She shook her head. "That stuff's for kids," she said. "The grownups like my nonfat caffaccino lattamocha. Want to try it?"

Kane gritted his teeth and lowered his head. Then he ran right at the zombie queen, screaming.

Ms. Garrity easily knocked him away. Kane went flying into a huge sack of coffee beans.

"Ugh," Kane said, shaking his head.

"Enough of this," the lunch lady said. She ladled a cup of the drink into a mug and walked toward Kane.

"Time for you to drink," she said. She leaned forward and grabbed Kane's cheeks, trying to force his mouth open.

Kane reached out with one hand and grabbed a handful of coffee beans. He threw them into the zombie queen's face. It shocked her, making her drop the mug.

"Why, you little . . . !" the lunch lady screamed.

Kane got to his feet and ran toward the vat of zombie drink. At the front door, the mob of zombies shrieked and moaned.

"I'll get you for that," Ms. Garrity said. She ran toward him, ready to grab him, but Kane stepped aside at the last moment.

The zombie queen went tumbling past him, right into the vat of steaming liquid.

"No!" she screamed, trying to stay afloat.

Kane looked around for a lid, but found nothing. Instead, he grabbed a small table from nearby. He lifted it over his head.

"Table for two?" he asked with a smirk. Then he dropped it upside down over the vat like a cover. The zombie queen was trapped in her own concoction.

Finally, it was quiet. Kane found a chair and sat down to catch his breath. He looked at the mob of zombies at the front door as they collapsed to the sidewalk. After a few minutes, they began to stand up. Right in the front was his mother, and she knew him.

Case number: 16778

Date reported: January 2

Crime scene: Ravens Pass Middle School; downtown Ravens Pass

Local police: All were affected

Civilian witnesses: Kane Tuttle, age 12; Mortimer Entwhistle, age unknown

Disturbance: Zombie uprising, beginning at two locations in town: the middle school and the coffee shop.

Suspect information: The first zombie uprising in Ravens Pass was in 1911. A hundred years later, Bridget O'Garrity, also known as the Garrity Zombie, returned. She is a zombie queen, and while she's currently in a state of limbo, she has not been defeated for good.

CASE NOTES:

I WAS CALLED IN AROUND 11 A.M. ON THE DAY OF THE UPRISING AFTER CITIZENS AROUND TOWN WERE AFFECTED. SOON, I WAS SURE I WAS THE ONLY PERSON WHO HADN'T BEEN TURNED. THE SCHOOLS HAD ALL BEEN INFECTED. I'D HEARD OF THE O'GARRITY UPRISING BACK IN 1911, BUT WE ALL THOUGHT THAT THE GARRITY ZOMBIE HAD BEEN DEFEATED THEN.

MY FIRST STOP AFTER SEEING THE DESTRUCTION DOWNTOWN WAS MORTIMER ENTWHISTLE'S CABIN IN RAVENSWOOD FOREST. HE'D HAD A VISIT FROM KANE TUTTLE. TUTTLE WAS ALREADY GONE, AND I SET OFF AFTER HIM. BY THE TIME I GOT BACK TO TOWN, THE QUEEN HAD BEEN CAPTURED.

MY HOPE IS THAT IT'S FOR GOOD. BUT NO ONE CAN SAY FOR SURE. AFTER ALL, WE THOUGHT SHE WAS DEFEATED IN 1911.

DEAR READER,

THEY ASKED ME TO WRITE ABOUT MYSELF. THE FIRST THING YOU NEED TO KNOW IS THAT JASON STRANGE IS NOT MY REAL NAME. IT'S A NAME I'VE TAKEN TO HIDE MY TRUE IDENTITY AND PROTECT THE PEOPLE I CARE ABOUT.

YOU WOULDN'T BELIEVE THE THINGS I'VE SEEN, WHAT I'VE WITNESSED. IF PEOPLE KNEW I WAS TELLING THESE STORIES, SHARING THEM WITH THE WORLD, THEY'D TRY TO GET ME TO STOP. BUT THESE STORIES NEED TO BE TOLD, AND I'M THE ONLY ONE WHO CAN TELL THEM.

I CAN'T TELL YOU MANY DETAILS ABOUT MY LIFE. I CAN TELL YOU I WAS BORN IN A SMALL TOWN AND LIVE IN ONE STILL. I CAN TELL YOU I WAS A POLICE DETECTIVE HERE FOR TWENTY-FIVE YEARS BEFORE I RETIRED. I CAN TELL YOU I'M STILL OUT THERE EVERY DAY AND THAT CRAZY THINGS ARE STILL HAPPENING.

I'LL LEAVE YOU WITH ONE QUESTION—IS ANY OF THIS TRUE?

JASON STRANGE
RAVENS PASS

Glossary

allergic (uh-LUR-jik)—if you are allergic to something, it makes you sick when you inhale or eat it

chaos (KAY-oss)—total confusion

confusion (kuhn-FYOO-zhuhn)—a feeling of not understanding

eerie (IHR-ee)—strange and frightening, creepy

figure (FIG-yur)—a person's shape

gruel (GROOL)—a thin, liquid food of oatmeal or other meal boiled in milk or water

hermit (HUR-mit)—someone who lives alone and away from other people

horde (HORD)—a large, noisy, moving group

infect (in-FEKT)—to cause disease

lone (LOHN)—alone

lumbering (LUHM-bur-ing)—moving heavily and clumsily

transformation (transs-for-MAY-shuhn)—change

uprising (UHP-rye-zing)—a rebellion or revolt

DISCUSSION QUESTIONS

1. Why did the zombie queen want to turn the townspeople into zombies?

2. Mortimer lives all alone in the woods. If you lived all alone, how would you spend your time?

3. What was the creepiest part of this book? Explain your answer.

WRITING PROMPTS

1. Winter is long in Ravens Pass. What is your favorite season? Write about it.

2. This is a horror story. Write your own horror story.

3. Kane is allergic to chocolate. What would be the worst thing for you to be allergic to? Why?